The Big, Bad City

Written and Illustrated by Shoo Rayner

Collins

"Granny said her house was easy to find," sighed Little Red Hen. "But this map just doesn't make sense!"

"Can I help?" asked a smiley stranger.

"Granny told me not to speak to strangers," said Little Red Hen.

"I can't be a stranger!" he laughed. "I live around here. My name is Mr Fox and I know this city like the back of my paw!"

That seemed to make everything all right.

"Well, Granny told me to go north from the station and follow the signs to Main Street," Little Red Hen explained. "Granny lives above the book shop, but I can't find Main Street on the map."

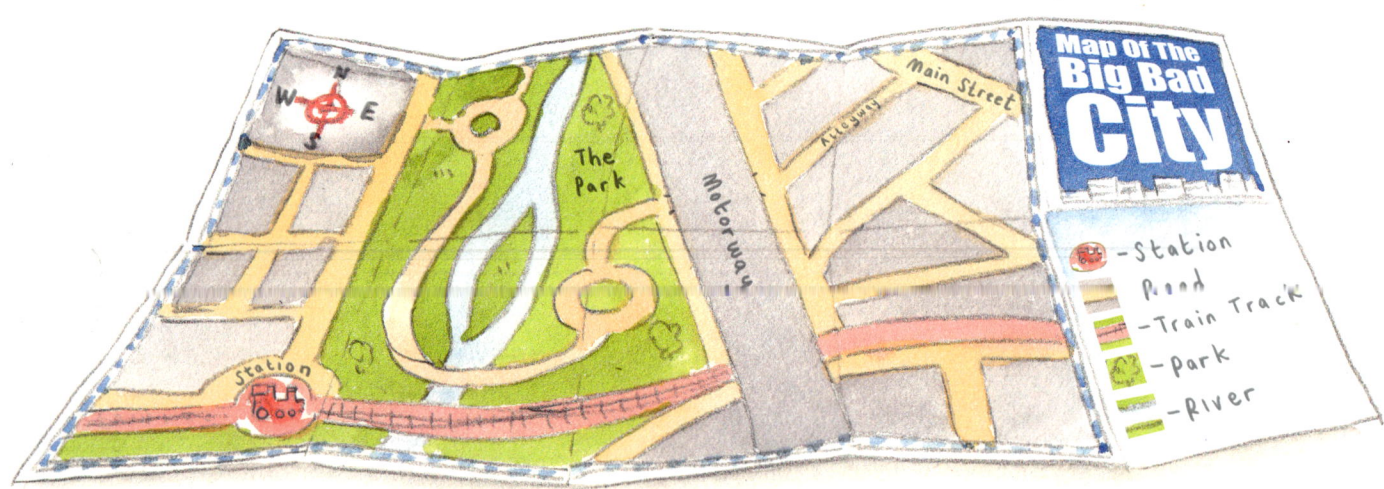

"Don't worry, I know a short cut!" Mr Fox smiled. "It's much quicker. But stay close. You must be very careful in this big, bad city!"

"Granny says that too!"
said Little Red Hen, nervously.

Mr Fox led the way through the park.
The path twisted in and out of the tall trees.

"There are too many people here!" Mr Fox grumbled.

"They're all having picnics in the sunshine," said Little Red Hen.

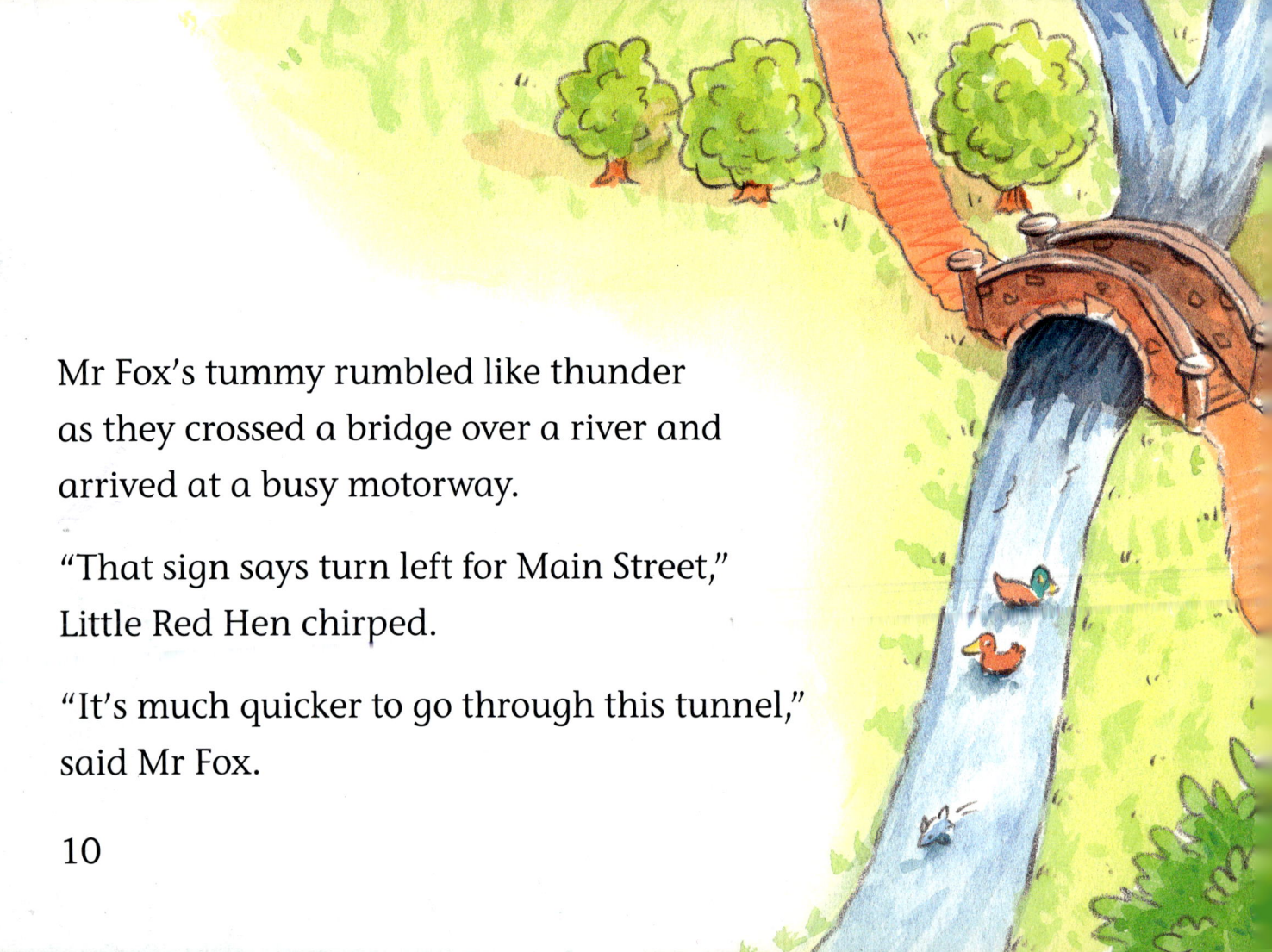

Mr Fox's tummy rumbled like thunder as they crossed a bridge over a river and arrived at a busy motorway.

"That sign says turn left for Main Street," Little Red Hen chirped.

"It's much quicker to go through this tunnel," said Mr Fox.

"Don't worry," said Mr Fox.
"I can see really well in the dark.
Stay close and follow me."

Someone in the tunnel began to sing.

"Bother!" said Mr Fox. "I thought no one used this tunnel!"

"It was a lovely song," said Little Red Hen.
She blinked in the sunlight as they came out of the tunnel.

Mr Fox's tummy rumbled, loudly.
"We turn left down this alley," he said.

Little Red Hen pointed ahead. "But that sign says turn right for Main Street."

Mr Fox shook his head.
"This way is much quicker."

Little Red Hen stopped and studied her map.

Mr Fox smiled, licked his lips and …

"Here's the alley on the map!"
Little Red Hen squawked.
"So that must be Main Street over there!"

She skipped to the end of the alley as fast as her little legs would go.

"Oh look!" Little Red Hen panted, as people bustled past her on Main Street.
"There's Granny's flat, above the book shop!"

"Oh, bother!" sighed Mr Fox.
"I mean ... Oh, perfect!"

"Thank you," said Little Red Hen. "Your shortcut was much quicker. You really do know this city like the back of your paw. I hope I meet you the next time I get lost."

Mr Fox rubbed his rumbling tummy. "Next time," he grumbled, "I'll show you an even quicker way!"

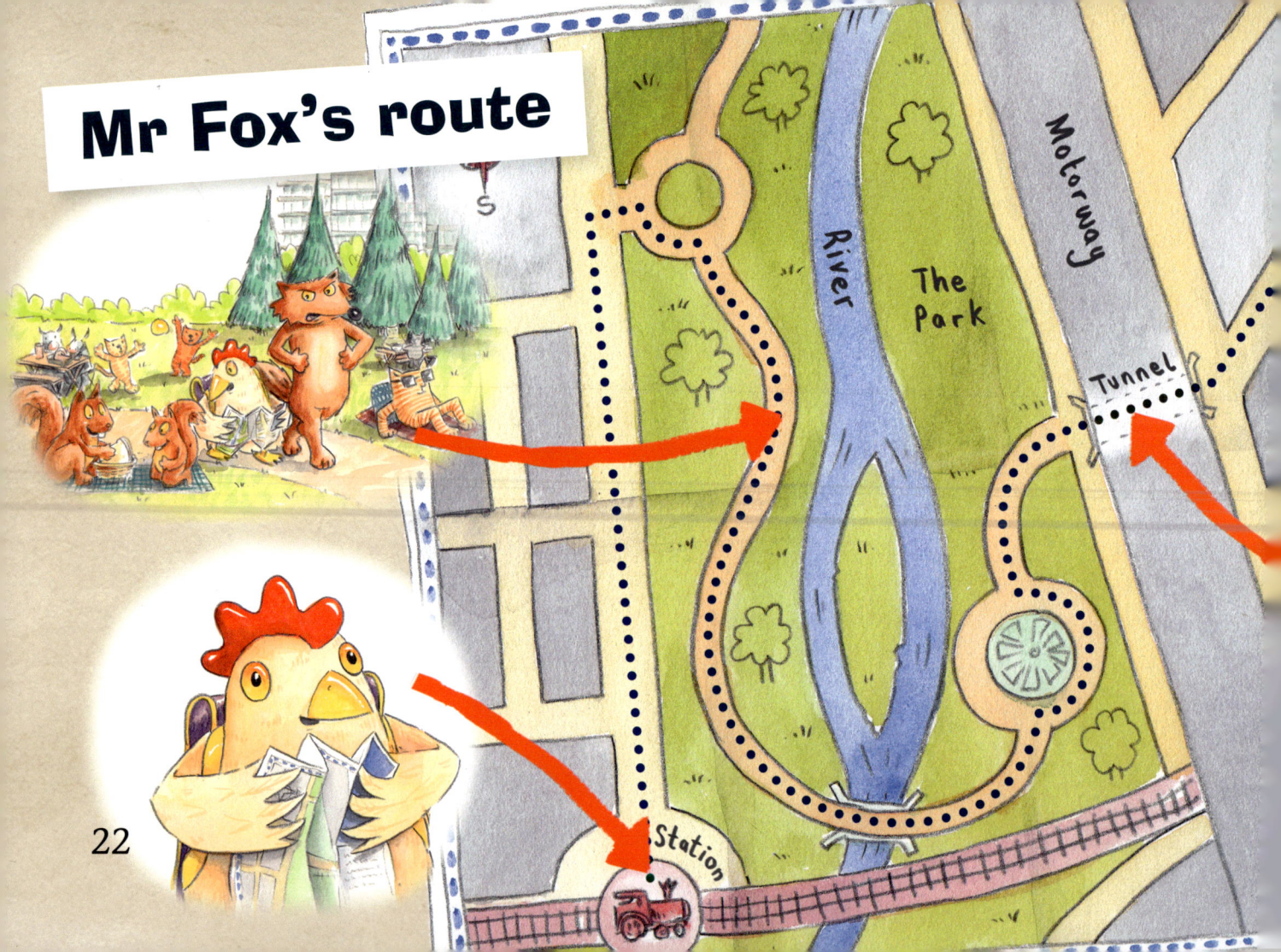

Ideas for reading

Written by Clare Dowdall, PhD
Lecturer and Primary Literacy Consultant

Learning objectives: read aloud books closely matched to improving phonic knowledge, sounding out unfamiliar words accurately, automatically and without undue hesitation; discuss and clarify the meanings of words, linking new meanings to known vocabulary; use spoken language to develop understanding through speculating, hypothesising, imagining and exploring ideas

Curriculum links: Geography

Interest words: stranger, sighed, laughed, explained, rumbled, chirped, squawked, panted, sighed, grumbled

Word count: 453

Resources: pens and paper for making a poster, local maps or ICT-based map

Getting started

This book can be read over two or more reading sessions.

- Look at the front cover. Help children to identify who the creatures are, what they are doing, and what the title *Big Bad City* suggests about the story, e.g. something bad could happen.
- Read the blurb aloud together. Ask children to explain what a stranger is, and whether they think Little Red Hen should trust the smiley stranger. Challenge children to think about why he is a *smiley* stranger.

Reading and responding

- Turn to pp 2–3. Model reading the text to the children, using an expressive voice for each character.